Forest Folk Tales

Forest Folk Tales

Fables and Parables From God's Great Outdoors

by

MARIAN M. SCHOOLLAND

AUTHOR OF

Marian's Favorite Bible Stories,
Marian's Big Book of Bible Stories, etc.

Illustrations by

REYNOLD H. WEIDENAAR

WM. B. EERDMANS PUBLISHING COMPANY
Grand Rapids   Michigan

Set up and printed, March 1952
Sixth printing, April 1974

ISBN 0-8028-4030-2

PRINTED IN THE UNITED STATES OF AMERICA

To
my dear niece
WILLAINE

In every forest of the land,
  If you will only look,
You'll find the little Forest Folk,
  The people of this book.

They do not speak our language.
They're shy; they'll hide from you.
    But if you're quiet,
    If you're kind,
    And if you listen well,
There are stories of obedience,
And faith, and trust, they tell.

We Meet the Forest Folk

The Forest seems to be a very quiet place. When you take a walk in The Forest you seldom see anyone at all. If you did not know better, you would surely think no one lived there.

But as you walk along the shady path and look around, you may be sure that bright eyes are watching you every minute. Bright eyes are peeping from behind the leaves of the big trees, from dark doorways of hollow logs, from snug nests in the low bushes, and from the cool shade of tall grasses. The Forest Folk see you, even though you do not see them.

As soon as you are gone, the Forest Folk come out of their hiding places, and maybe they laugh about you because they have fooled you. But they haven't much time to laugh; they are busy folk. Before you have gone very far, they are at their work again. And what a busy place The Forest is then! Why, there's a lot of work going on — hammering and digging and fishing and weaving. There are cows to be milked and babies to be fed. If you could see all the Forest Folk — all the tiny ones, as well as the middle sized ones, and the big ones — you would agree that The Forest is almost as busy and as crowded as one of our big cities!

But since the Forest Folk hide when they hear you come, you may like to read about them — about the things they do, and how they make their living. The stories of this book also tell what they might say to each other if they could talk, and how they might act if they were like you and me. The Forest Folk have their fun and their troubles; they make mistakes, too, just as we do. Maybe we can learn some very good lessons from them.

There are so many Forest Folk that we cannot put them all into one little book. We have had to choose just a few for these stories, and they are:

Johnny Woodchuck and Bunny Rabbit
The Busy Bees
Polly Wog and Silver Fish
The Whitefoot Family
Flutterwing and Mrs. Chipmunk
Mr. and Mrs. Redbreast
Elsie Redbreast
Some Foolish Little Folk with Wings
Little Fifth Chickadee
Reddy, the Squirrel

And last of all,
Crickie, the Violinist

And then, in
Who's Afraid?
we shall tell a little about the Forest Folk in winter.

M. M. S.

Contents

Illustrations

Forest Folk Tales

1

Johnny Woodchuck and Bunny Rabbit

IT WAS spring time, and The Forest was a lovely place. The ground was dotted with flowers,
pink ones and blue ones. The birds were singing
in the tree tops. And the animals were all scurry-
ing around, either playing or working. They were
happy because at last the long winter was past.

Bunny Rabbit was so happy that he tried to turn
somersaults, just as Reddy the squirrel often does
when he is bubbling over with fun. But Bunny
Rabbit is not as quick on his feet as Reddy. The
best he could do was kick high, and jump sideways
now and then.

Now Bunny Rabbit was on his way to Farmer
Duff's garden; he hoped to find some fresh vegetables just peeking above the ground, and was sure
Farmer Duff would not mind sharing them with
the Bunny family. But as he came near the creek,
he heard the queerest grunting and puffing. It
sounded as if someone was in great trouble.

Very carefully Bunny Rabbit peeked over the
edge of the creek bank, for the noise seemed to come
from there. And in a minute he knew that Johnny

Woodchuck was doing the grunting and puffing. Johnny's hole was right there, half-way down the creek bank.

"What's the matter, Johnny?" Bunny Rabbit called.

The grunting and puffing stopped for just a moment. Johnny came backing out of his hole, to look up at Bunny Rabbit. But instead of answering Bunny Rabbit's question, Johnny only went back into his hole and started grunting and puffing again.

"Can I help you?" Bunny Rabbit asked, hopping a little closer.

Once more the grunting and puffing stopped, while Johnny backed out of his den. This time he sat back and looked at Bunny Rabbit and said crossly, "It's the old creek. The water came so high last week that it ran right into my doorway and washed my living room full of mud. Now I can dig the whole place out again. It was a good den, and there's nothing more provoking than to have it ruined this way. I worked hard making it just right."

Bunny Rabbit sighed. "That is a pity," he said. And because he couldn't think of anything else to say, he sat back on his haunches and watched. He was sorry poor Johnny's home was ruined.

Building a home like Johnny Woodchuck's is hard work. The creek bank is hard-packed sand, full of roots, and Johnny has only his feet to dig with.

He started to dig at the sand by his doorway, now.

Bunny watched the sand fly for a few minutes, and then said, "I would help you if I could."

Johnny grumbled and grunted, and then said, "Thanks, Bunny. I guess it's my job. Anyway, you couldn't do it as well as I can."

"Well, I'll drop by later to see how you are getting along," Bunny said, and he hopped off in the direction of Farmer Duff's garden.

But he was only two hops from Johnny's den when he stopped. He had thought of something, and he turned to hop back.

Johnny's nose was deep inside the doorway, and his hind feet were kicking out the sand. Only his short tail showed. But when he heard Bunny call, he came out to see why Bunny was back so soon.

"I just happened to think of something to make your work easier," Bunny said.

Johnny looked at Bunny with bright eyes, and wiped the sand off his whiskers with one paw. But he growled crossly.

"What do you know about wookchuck burrows?" he asked.

"Nothing," Bunny Rabbit admitted quickly. "But I know something about work. I know that when there's something hard to be done, it gets done easier and quicker if its done cheerfully."

"Cheerfully!" Johnny exploded with anger. "Don't tell me to be cheerful when I've got a job like this! I wonder if you would be cheerful if

"What do *you* know about Woodchuck burrows?" Johnny growled.

your house was full of mud . . .!" And he kicked
a lump of wet sand toward Bunny.

Bunny Rabbit dodged the lump of sand, and
called over his shoulder as he hopped away, "I only
meant to help!"

An hour later Bunny Rabbit, on his way back
from Farmer Duff's garden, stopped to peek down
the bank at Johnny again. He did not call "Hello!"
for fear Johnny might still be angry.

But Johnny was not in sight.

Very cautiously, Bunny Rabbit crept down the
bank and peeked into Johnny Woodchuck's doorway. It was a neat round hole, and the sand Johnny
had kicked out lay in a neat pile beside it. A big
root of the basswood tree sheltered the hole from
the north wind.

Bunny put his nose inside the hole and sniffed.
It was pitch dark in there, but Bunny could smell
Johnny. He crept in a little farther, and then stood
still in surprise. He heard something, and it didn't
sound one bit like Johnny's voice. It was a cheery
whistle, a merry tune! And then Bunny heard
shuffling feet.

Bunny backed out, and stopped at a safe distance.
When he looked again, Johnny was in the doorway,
looking very cheerful. He saw Bunny Rabbit.

"Well, glad to see you back so soon!" he called.

"Was that you whistling?" Bunny asked. He
could hardly believe it.

"Of course it was!" said Johnny. "Most folks don't know that we woodchucks can whistle; we do it only in our own homes. But I want to tell you that I followed your advice, and it helped. You should see my burrow now! I'm right proud of it! Won't you come in and see it?"

Bunny was glad to go, and followed Johnny through the dark doorway. The hall slanted downward for about three feet, and Bunny was just getting used to the slope when he found himself groping upward.

"What's the idea of digging downward first, and then upward?" he asked.

"Wait and see," Johnny answered, and led on. Soon they came out into a little room, cozy and snug as could be.

"A perfect place for a nest!" Bunny Rabbit exclaimed.

Johnny nodded, proudly. "And it will stay dry," he said. "You see, if I dug downward and put my nest at the bottom of the tunnel, the rain would come washing down and drown us out. But now the rain can run down and drain away, and we'll be safe and dry up on this higher level."

"Of course," said Bunny Rabbit. "That's very wise. But where did you learn that trick?"

"Learn it?" Johnny echoed. "I didn't learn it, really. You know, Bunny, that each of us has been given the wisdom we need to do the work we should do. Our Creator saw to that. After you left me a while ago, I got to thinking about those things, and I began to feel thankful, and then cheerful. And then the work wasn't hard at all."

Bunny Rabbit nodded. "You are right, Johnny," he said.

And as he hurried on home to feed his babies, he kept thinking about it; he had taught Johnny a lesson, but Johnny had reminded him of one, too.

"I have my work to do, and Johnny has his," he told himself as he hopped along. "I can't do Johnny's and he can't do mine, but each of us can do his own, and can do it cheerfully."

2

The Busy Bees

FOR a few days in early summer The Forest was fragrant with a very sweet perfume. Most of the spring flowers were gone, and you might have hunted and hunted to find the blossoms from which that fragrance came. Perhaps you would not find them at all by looking; but you would surely find them by listening.

The fragrance came from the big basswood tree. Its tall crown, high among the forest trees, was full of tiny fuzzy whitish-yellow blossoms. The bees had discovered them as soon as the first petals had unfolded, and from morning till night they hummed happily in the basswood tree, busy gathering nectar and pollen from the tiny flowers.

It is the humming of the bees, that helps you find the fragrant tree.

Bunny Rabbit was not interested in the blossoms of the basswood tree, but he sat under it one day to rest. He hardly noticed the cheerful humming of the busy bees above his head. But suddenly he heard two bee voices that were not cheerful.

"We are tired of feeding the drones while they do nothing."

"I won't do another bit of work until they work, too!" one little bee voice said, and sounded very cross.

"That's the way I feel," said the other. "They are just lazy; they stay at home all day, just flitting around the queen and taking life easy."

The first added, "They don't gather even enough honey to feed themselves, but they feast on the honey we bring in."

"Yet the queen says she needs them," said the second. "She could send them away, if she wanted to — or command us to chase them out."

Bunny Rabbit moved a little, rustling the dry leaves. He did not want to be an eavesdropper, so he tried to let the bees know he was there.

As soon as they heard Bunny Rabbit, and saw him, the two unhappy bees came flying down to a tall grass blade near him.

"Oh, Bunny Rabbit," said the first one, "maybe you can tell us what to do. You see, at our hive there are some bees who do not work at all, and we think it's quite unfair. We don't want to work unless they do their share. Can you tell us how to make them do their part? Or how to get rid of them if they won't work?"

Bunny Rabbit wriggled his long ears thoughtfully. "It's none of my business, really," he said. "But I have heard about those lazy fellows before. They are the drones of the hive, I think."

"Yes, they are the drones," said the second bee. "And we are tired of feeding them while they do nothing."

"It does seem unfair," Bunny Rabbit said. "But tell me a little about yourself and about the drones. Is it true that you have pollen baskets in which to gather pollen? And do you really have sharp stings with which to fight? And wax plates with which to make honey comb? And honey stomachs that you fill with nectar to carry to the hive? And is it true that this nectar, which you take from the flowers, is changed to honey in the comb?"

"All that is true!" said both bees. "We have really wonderful tools with which to do our work."

Then they showed Bunny Rabbit the little pollen baskets on their elbows — little baskets made of the tiny hairs on their legs. One bee had his stuffed full of pollen, to carry home to make bee bread for the bee children. The other lifted his wings to show the wax plates from which he can make honey comb.

"And is it true," Bunny Rabbit asked then, "that the drones do not have pollen baskets, or honey stomachs, or wax plates, or any of the tools you have for gathering pollen and nectar?"

"Yes, that is true, too!" said both bees. "The drones do not even have tongues long enough to reach the delicious nectar in the flowers!" And they both laughed.

But Bunny Rabbit said, "Then they cannot do the work you do."

At that both bees stopped laughing.

"That's true, too," said one. "They can't. If they could, maybe they would."

"Besides that," said Bunny Rabbit, "who are you working for? Are you obeying the drones? Or do you obey your queen?"

"We work for our queen, of course," said both bees.

Bunny Rabbit nodded. "I thought so," he said. "You are her servants. The drones are her servants, too. Don't you think . . ."

Bunny Rabbit didn't have to finish his sentence. Both bees said, "Oh, of course! We don't need to worry about what the drones do, or what they don't do! We will work faithfully for our queen, and do our very best. And our queen will reward each of us according to our deeds. She will drive out the drones when she is ready."

And as they flew off together, humming their merry bee tune, they called back, "Thank you, Bunny Rabbit!"

3

Polly Wog and Silver Fish

THE pool was a favorite spot in The Forest. All the animals came to drink its cool spring-fed waters. During the day the birds came to bathe along its shallow edge, and a pretty little fawn often came to look at its own reflection in the dark mirror.

Bunny Rabbit liked the pool, too. The grass around it was green and delicious, and there were other plants good to eat. Sometimes he liked to sit quietly under a green shrub and look at the blue blossoms of the pickerel weed along the water's edge, and at the water lilies that bobbed up and down on the ripples. It was cool there; and because The Forest was dense all around, he felt safe and happy.

One warm June day Bunny Rabbit sat there, resting from a long run, and he saw a glint of silver flash through the dark waters.

"A fish!" he said to himself, and he went closer to watch the graceful silver fish dart under the leaves of a nearby pickerel weed. When he leaned over to see better, Bunny Rabbit saw a little black pollywog resting there, too. The pickerel weed made a cool, shady spot in the water garden.

Polly happened to look up, and saw Bunny Rabbit.

Now nobody is afraid of good Bunny Rabbit, so Polly called, "Hi, there! Why don't you come and join us here, where it's nice and cool!"

Bunny wrinkled his nose in a grin. "You know I can't," he said. "I wasn't made to live in water."

"That's right," said Polly. "But some day I shall be coming to live up there on land, with you!"

"What?" Bunny Rabbit exclaimed in surprise. "What did you say?"

Silver Fish was swimming by just then, and he stopped to ask the same question, "What was that you said?"

"I said that some day I'll be living up there, in the world of sunshine and trees," said Polly.

Silver Fish shook his fins and turned an easy somersault in the water. "Ha, ha!" he laughed. "Don't you wish it were true!"

"It is true," Polly answered seriously — so seriously that Silver Fish stared at him.

"Why, it's a silly idea," he said when he saw that Polly really meant what he said. "You are made to live in water, just as I am. You can't live up there, in the air. You'd choke to death!"

Polly smiled, without becoming one bit excited. He breathed quietly through his little gills and flicked his fat tail.

"Some day," he said, "this tail of mine will be gone and I'll have four legs like any animal that lives up there. And these gills will change into lungs, so that I'll be able to breathe air. I'll be made over entirely, and be able to live up there in the sunshine and fresh air."

"Impossible!" said Silver Fish. "That's just wishful thinking, Polly."

"I know it seems impossible," Polly admitted. "But I believe it, just the same."

Silver Fish turned to Bunny Rabbit. "You are a wise Bunny," he said. "You tell Polly what you think of his foolish notion."

Bunny Rabbit did not answer right away. He sat blinking and thinking. It did seem impossible, utterly impossible, that Polly should change so much that he could live up on land and breathe air. He was certainly made to live in water, with gills for breathing and a tail for swimming. Yet Bunny had heard of such things. Frogs living near the pool said they used to be tadpoles.

"It may be true, Silver Fish," he said at last. "Remember, there are many, many things that we cannot understand at all. In fact, we can't really explain anything — how we were made or why we were made to live as we do. One thing I know — He that made us can do anything He wants to with us. He can make us over, too, if He wants to. And if He has promised, He surely will. Nothing is too hard for Him."

Silver Fish flipped his fins and swished his tail. "Some people certainly are gullible. I, for one, can't believe it," he said. "I'll have to see Polly jump up on land before I'll believe that's possible." And he swam away scornfully.

"One day I knew I should jump out of the water, and here I am."

A few weeks later Bunny Rabbit happened to be close to the pool again. And as he nosed here and there for good bites to eat, he came upon a little green frog who greeted him with a pleasant croak.

"I'm very glad to see you again," said the little frog.

"I don't remember ever seeing you before," Bunny Rabbit answered.

Then the little green frog smiled from ear to ear. "I'm Polly," he said. "Do you remember talking with me and Silver Fish?"

Of course Bunny Rabbit remembered. But he would never have recognized Polly — the little fellow had changed so much.

"It happened just as I said it would," he said. "First I grew a pair of front legs; and after a while my tail sort of disappeared and hind legs grew under my skin. And my gills have changed to lungs, so that I breathe air. I can't tell how it all came about, but one day I knew I should jump out of the water. And here I am."

"Well," said Bunny Rabbit, "I can't explain it, either. But I'll say this — you are a living example to us that we should not try to limit God to the things that seem possible to us."

And as he hopped away, Polly croaked contentedly. "I can't understand it," he said half aloud, "but here I am!"

4

The Whitefoot Family

MOTHER Whitefoot is small and furry and grey. You can see at a glance that she belongs to the mouse tribe. But she is prettier and daintier than most of the mice. Her fur is softer and finer, her feet are pinkish white, and her ears are so big that she looks much like a tiny deer. She is gentle, too, and has a sweet musical voice.

The Whitefoot Family of The Forest had their home in a hollow tree, where there was a good cupboard for storing beechnuts. In spring Mother Whitefoot had lined the hole with fur and moss, so that it was a comfortable bed for her babies. And there her four little children were growing up — Johnny, Bobby, Sally and Lolly.

Now children of the Forest Folk are usually very obedient, as all children should be. Mother always knows what is best. So the four Whitefoot babies lay very quiet each time Mother left them alone, simply because she told them to.

But one day Mother stayed away longer than usual. Perhaps it was hard to find enough food that day. And the four Whitefoot children lay still till they could hardly lie still a minute longer.

"It seems to me we are big enough to get out of this stuffy nest and see the world," Bobby, the littlest of them all, whispered. And he moved carefully up to the doorway to look out.

"You mustn't do that!" sister Sally cried softly. "Stay down here!"

But Bobby saw something interesting, and turned with shining eyes to whisper, "Come up and see!"

Then they all climbed up to peek out.

On the ground below them there was a furry brown animal, much bigger than Mother. He had a long body and short legs, a sharp nose, and very bright eyes. He was sniffing the ground right at the bottom of their tree.

The little Whitefoot children felt their hearts beat very fast. And while they were looking, the furry brown animal began to talk. The four Whitefoot children turned their little big ears to catch every word.

"I'm sure Mrs. Whitefoot's nest is near here," he was saying. "My nose tells me so. I smell her nice cozy nest. But the nest is hard to find. If I could only let the Whitefoot children know that I want to play with them, I'm sure they would come out. And what fun we would have! Their mother would be glad too, because she knows they are safe with me, and she wants them to have a good time."

The Whitefoot babies looked at each other with big bright eyes. What fun it would be to climb out of this stuffy old nest and play with that big furry

Wally Weasel patiently waited for his prey.

fellow! And why not, if he was a friend of Mother's?

Bobby moved a little, as if he were ready to climb out. He even opened his mouth to call out, "Here we are, right up here in the hollow tree!" But just then there was a very soft rustle, and Mother Whitefoot was right there in the nest with them! She had come so quietly, using the back doorway, that they had not heard her at all. But how worried and afraid she looked! With one soft little sound she called them all to her. When she had nestled them close around her, they could feel her heart beating very fast.

They could not imagine what had frightened her, but they lay very still, knowing there was some danger near. At last Mother Whitefoot moved a little, and that was a sign that they might move, too.

"Wally Weasel was looking for you," she explained in a soft whisper. And, after stretching to look out the doorway, she added, "He's gone now, and we should be very thankful."

"Who is Wally Weasel, mother?" Bobby asked. "And what would he want us for?"

"Wally Weasel is a brown furry animal, much bigger than a mouse, with a long body and short legs and a sharp nose and . . ."

"But mother!" Johnny burst out, "we saw him, and he wanted us to come out and play, and he said he was a friend of yours — or at least he said you wouldn't mind if we played with him, because he would take good care of us!"

"Take very good care of you, indeed!" said Mother Whitefoot. "He would take you to his den, every one of you, and you would never, never get out again."

"But he seemed very nice," said Bobby, pouting. "And this old nest is so stuffy, and we get tired of waiting."

Then Mother Whitefoot set her four children in a row and gave them a lesson in obedience.

"You children are too young to know what is best for you," she said sternly. "If you had so much as squeaked, and Wally had heard you, not one of you would have been left to tell what happened."

Mother looked so serious that the children were all frightened.

"Wally is a deceiver," Mother went on. "Evil usually tempts us by pretending to be pleasant and good, and Wally is like that. Believe me, he would have eaten every one of you alive. Don't ever, ever listen to anyone who tells you to disobey your parents. Whoever tells you that, can never be right."

She looked from one to the other, and Lolly said, "Bobby was all ready to go when you came."

But Johnny did not want Bobby to have all the blame. He said, "We all would have followed him, I guess."

Mother Whitefoot said gently, "I understand. Evil tempts us all by its promise of fun and good times. It is a blessing that children have parents who know what is good for them."

"We'll obey you next time, mother," said Johnny.

"And lie very still while you're gone," said Bobby.

"And not listen when anyone tells us to disobey," said Sally.

"And then we'll all be happy," said Lolly.

"Yes," said Mother. "I hope you have learned your lesson. Now I must run out and pick up the package of nuts I left out in the grass. I dropped it in fright when I saw Wally. Then we shall have a good dinner together."

5

Flutterwing and Mrs. Chipmunk

IT WAS midsummer, and because the Chipmunk children were grown up and able to take care of themselves, Mrs. Chipmunk had time to take life a bit easy. When she did not have anything else to do, she sat in her doorway and watched her neighbors. And how she liked to find fault with them!

One day as Mrs. Chipmunk sat resting in the shade, Flutterwing happened by.

She didn't stop, but floated by as if on a breeze. And as Mrs. Chipmunk watched her go she muttered, "Lazy as ever. That butterfly is of no use at all, that I can see."

Flutterwing drifted to the little forest glade where the Queen Ann's Lace blossomed, and alighted gently upon the largest of the white blossoms. Mrs. Chipmunk watched her, and had to admit that she made a pretty picture, perched there on the flower. She was as dainty and delicate as the flower itself. Her orange and black wings seemed more beautiful than ever against the white of the blossom.

"But beauty is all she has," Mrs. Chipmunk said half aloud, and she turned up her nose. "I'd rather be plain and useful."

Mrs. Chipmunk watched her and had to admit that
she made a pretty picture.

Just then a high thin voice startled Mrs. Chipmunk so that she turned around with a jerk. It
was Blackie, the biggest of the black ants. He had

stopped to rest, because of the big burden he was pulling.

"How you startled me!" said Mrs. Chipmunk. "What was it you said?"

"I said," Blackie spoke in a scornful voice, "I said, please tell me, in what way are *you* so useful?"

"Why, what a question!" Mrs. Chipmunk exclaimed angrily. "How dare you ask that? You know very well that Mr. Chipmunk and I have worked hard, these many weeks, raising our family. And you know, too, that butterflies never pay one bit of attention to their babies. They merely lay their eggs, and go away; and they never come back to see if their babies are faring well and have enough to eat."

Blackie ran one of his feelers over his eyes. He was weary.

"I'll admit your babies would die if you neglected them," he said. "But butterfly babies get along very well without help. Mrs. Butterfly always makes sure she lays her eggs where the right food is plentiful. So you have no right to judge her. But if you don't do anything more than just feed your family, I don't think you are really being useful. At least that isn't what I mean by being useful."

"Then what do you mean?" Mrs. Chipmunk asked.

Blackie thought a moment and answered, "I really can't quite say. It just seems to me we ought to do

more than just live for ourselves and our families.
I don't quite know what . . ."

"Oh, you are talking nonsense," said Mrs. Chipmunk. "I don't want to listen to you." And with
an angry frisk of her tail she turned away and ran
into her den.

Blackie stood still a moment longer, wondering if
what he had said to Mrs. Chipmunk was not true
of himself, too! What did he do, besides taking
care of his family?

"I guess I'm not really of much use, either," he
sighed. "Of course we have to take care of our families, but . . ."

He could not quite figure it out. But he took up
his burden and moved slowly on toward home.

When she was sure he was gone, Mrs. Chipmunk
came out again. The weather was much too nice;
she did not want to stay inside her stuffy den. But
she stopped suddenly in the doorway, because The
Boy was there. The Girl was with him, and they
were walking toward the little forest glade where
Flutterwing was flitting from flower to flower.

Mrs. Chipmunk was afraid of what might hap-
pen to Flutterwing when she heard The Girl ex-
claim, "Look at the pretty butterfly!"

"Shall I catch it for you?" The Boy asked.

But The Girl said, "Oh, no! You might hurt it.
Instead, let's see how near to it we can get, so we
can see how it sips nectar from the flowers.'"

So The Boy and The Girl walked on, ever so quietly, toward the glade. And The Girl said, softly, "The Forest is very quiet. Do you suppose all the Forest Folk are asleep?"

She did not know that Mrs. Chipmunk was watching from her doorway, and Reddy was watching from his perch in the tree, and Redbreast was peeking over the edge of her nest in the crotch of the wild crab-apple, and Polly was spying from under a leaf at the edge of the pool.

They walked so carefully that Flutterwing did not see them come. Or if she did see them, she was not afraid. She flitted to a milkweed blossom very near to The Boy and The Girl, and she uncurled her long tongue to get the nectar hidden deep inside the milkweed flower.

The Boy and The Girl watched. They saw the wonder of the frail wings, the velvety softness of the black body with its white polka-dots, the slender tongue that uncurled and dipped into the blossoms, the shining black eyes, the dainty feet, the sensitive feelers . . .

"What a wonderful creature!" The Boy said softly, watching Flutterwing with admiring eyes.

"Yes," The Girl answered even more softly. "It is so frail, and so delicate, and so beautiful! And it is alive! Nobody can understand the wonder of such a little creature being alive! When you think of all that, you cannot help but praise God, who made the pretty butterfly."

The Boy nodded, and they stood watching Flutterwing till she drifted away in the breeze to find another glade and other blossoms.

When The Boy and The Girl were gone, Mrs. Chipmunk sat very still, thinking hard.

"Flutterwing is wonderful!" she told herself. "Why, just seeing her makes people praise God! I guess she is useful that way; for anything that brings praise to God is worthwhile. It doesn't have to be great deeds; it can be just a beautiful life!"

She was still sitting there when Blackie came by again, hurrying to get another load. He stopped when Mrs. Chipmunk called him.

Mrs. Chipmunk told him about The Boy and The Girl, and what she thought of Flutterwing's usefulness after hearing The Boy and The Girl talk.

"I think you are right," said Blackie, rubbing one antenna over his eyes. "That's being useful. And even I can try it! I can do things that make folks praise my Maker, too!"

6

Mr. and Mrs. Redbreast

MR. AND MRS. Redbreast had built a strong nest in the wild crab-apple tree; Mrs. Redbreast had laid four robin-blue eggs and brooded them faithfully. Now there were four babies, and it was a happy family.

Of course Mr. and Mrs. Redbreast were busy, with four hungry babies to feed. But there was never a shortage of food. There were plenty of worms and bugs under the leaves of The Forest's floor. And the babies were healthy; they grew stronger by the day. No wonder Mr. and Mrs. Redbreast were happy.

Early every morning Mr. Redbreast would fly to the top of the nearby tall elm tree to watch for the sunrise. And as soon as the splendor of the sun began to light the eastern sky, he would lift his head and sing a song of praise. Mrs. Redbreast, still hunched on the nest to keep her babies warm against the dampness of the dew, would cluck contentedly.

All the Forest Folk enjoyed hearing Mr. Redbreast sing his morning song — at least almost all.

The babies grew, but danger was always near.

His song reminded them that they, too, should begin each day with praise to God. If they could not sing, they could at least have thoughts of praise and thanksgiving.

The only one who did not feel that way was Wally Weasel. Wally did not have a song in his own heart, and it made him cross to see someone else happy.

"Anyway, it's easy enough for that bird to sing," he grumbled to his wife. "Mr. Redbreast is rich and prosperous, without a care in the world. I just wish a little trouble would come his way. Then he wouldn't have such a fine tune to sing."

Wally was not poor, and his children did not go hungry. But Wally had such a cross disposition that it annoyed him when others were prosperous and happy.

And one day trouble did come to the Redbreast family.

It was a sunny afternoon, and The Forest seemed very peaceful. But suddenly all the Forest Folk heard a scream of fright.

Mr. Redbreast was hunting food, but he recognized the voice that screamed. It was Mrs. Redbreast's! He dashed home at top speed, with other Forest Folk following him to see what was the matter. They came running and flying toward the crab-apple tree, from all directions. And they were just in time to see a big snake slither down out of the tree with a baby robin in its mouth.

"The last of my babies!" Mother Redbreast cried. "He got them all!" And she flew at the snake, to peck at him fiercely. But the snake did not mind one bit.

A dozen other birds were in the tree — jays, catbirds, phoebes, bluebirds, juncos, chickadees. They were all screaming, and they were all trembling with fear, but they could not help poor Mrs. Redbreast. The snake was so big, no one could stop him.

Bunny Rabbit was on the ground, watching too, and wishing he could do something to help. He was feeling very sorry for Mr. and Mrs. Redbreast, when suddenly a cheerful voice close to his ear said,

"Too bad, eh, Bunny Rabbit?"

Bunny Rabbit jumped at the sound of that voice. It was Wally Weasel right there next to him, and Bunny Rabbit knew very well that Wally would enjoy a rabbit supper. Besides, that cheerful voice made him angry.

"Yes, it is a pity," Bunny Rabbit said, and moved away a little. "How quickly trouble can come, and upset all our hopes and plans!"

"Quite so, quite so," Wally answered, grinning. "Every dog has his day. Poor Redbreast won't have anything to sing about tomorrow morning."

He started away then, and Bunny Rabbit watched him until he was out of sight. By that time most of the other Forest Folk had gone back to their business, talking excitedly about the terrible tragedy as they went. Up in the crab-apple tree, Mr.

and Mrs. Redbreast were hovering about their empty nest and calling to each other sadly.

"I just can't believe they are gone!" Mrs. Redbreast cried. "I had gathered a good mouthful of worms, and when I came to feed the poor dears, the snake was taking one of them."

Bunny could not bear to stay and listen, so he loped away. Poor Redbreast — so happy this morning, and now so sad. The Forest Folk would surely miss his song in the morning. Maybe it would be many mornings before Redbreast would sing again.

Noticing that the sun was already sinking toward the west, Bunny knew he must hurry to see if his babies were safe.

An hour later, when the setting sun was painting the western sky with glory, he happened to pass close to the crab-apple tree again. All was quiet there now, and the robins were gone.

Bunny hopped on, feeling very sad. But what was that? Someone singing like Mr. Robin Redbreast used to sing! Up there in the elm, where Redbreast always sang his morning songs! Why, it was Redbreast himself!

Staring in surprise, Bunny called to Reddy, the squirrel, "Is that Mr. Redbreast up there, singing?"

And Reddy called back, "Yes, it is! Doesn't his song seem lovelier than ever?"

It certainly did! And he was singing so wholeheartedly! The last rays of the sun shone on his red breast, and his little black head was thrown back to let the music roll out of his little throat.

Bunny Rabbit could hardly believe his big ears. While he stood listening, he was startled by a brown furry body moving in the long grass close by. It was Wally again!

"Don't be frightened," said Wally Weasel, when Bunny Rabbit started to run. "I'm not after you just now. I'm only trying to make sure that it's Mr. Robin Redbreast singing up there."

"It is," Bunny declared. "And isn't his song wonderful?"

"Humph," grunted Wally. But he added, "I must admit, though, that I'm surprised to hear him. I guess he didn't love his family so very much after all."

"Oh, but he did!" said Bunny.

"Well, then I don't understand how he can sing," said Wally.

"Neither do I," said Bunny, and he started to move away. But after one hop he turned and said, "Come to think of it, I do understand. We can always be happy if we remember that there is a Father in heaven who cares for us."

Wally Weasel's sharp eyes looked at Bunny curiously, and Bunny said, "If we know that He does what is best for His children, then even the biggest sorrows can't keep us from singing, for very long."

Wally shrugged his shoulders and walked away, while Bunny hopped off in the other direction.

"It isn't always easy," he said to himself, remembering that he and his family were often chased and hunted. But he was thankful for robins who can sing even when their hearts are heavy with sorrow.

7

Elsie Redbreast

A FEW days after the horror of the snake rob-
bery, Mr. and Mrs. Redbreast began building
a second nest. This time they chose the thorn-apple
tree near the pool as their home site.

Mrs. Redbreast worked hard, carrying mud and
straw. When she had enough, she shaped it with
her body — sitting in the little cup and turning
round and round until it was smooth as could be.
Sometimes she was quite a sight, for working in
mud does not improve one's clothes. And no matter how many baths she took in the pool, she could
not get her feathers to look bright and pretty again.
Besides that, she was thin and tired, for she had
worked hard building her first nest and raising her
first family.

The brooding days were peaceful days, and Mrs.
Robin enjoyed a good rest. But then followed weeks
of hard work again while the family grew up. Mr.
Redbreast helped faithfully; but with each child
eating its own weight in worms and bugs every day,
they had no time to rest, from dawn till dark. Mrs.
Redbreast was happy, though, and proud of the

four new babies who were growing up to be healthy youngsters. They were handsome too, and lively as could be.

Elsie, the liveliest of them all, seemed especially bright. Mrs. Redbreast noticed with pride how quickly she learned to keep herself clean and neat, even though she was still a nestling.

Mrs. Redbreast told Bunny Rabbit about Elsie one day, when she happened to meet him in the brush heap.

"Well, I'm certainly glad for you," said Bunny Rabbit. "I hope this bright child of yours may bring you much happiness. You've had so much trouble, and you've worked so hard."

"Oh, I haven't minded the work at all," said Mrs. Redbreast, cheerfully.

But when the children were almost big enough to leave the nest, Mrs. Redbreast became a bit worried. Elsie was turning out to be a sour-puss. She complained about most of the worms mother brought — they were too thin or too fat, too salty or too sweet, too juicy or not juicy enough. Elsie would turn away her bill and hardly take a nibble. She might have been quite weak and thin, except that when Mother brought an especially good grub or worm, she would snatch it before anyone else could get even a nibble.

Father Redbreast would sigh and say, "I'll be glad when she is out of the nest. Then she will find out that making a living isn't easy."

"She talks as if we were good-for-nothings," Mother said. "She says she is going to be 'somebody.' She is going to live a much better life than we do."

"She is a bright girl," said father. "But she will never be really happy unless she is good."

When the four children were at last old enough to leave the nest, Elsie quickly learned how to listen for grubs and worms, and how to pull them out of their hiding places. But she did not want to do such dirty work. She found a pleasant spot in Mrs. Duff's flower garden, and preened her feathers, and called mother to bring her a fat worm or a grub.

Mother spoiled Elsie. She brought her the best food she could find. She hoped that Elsie would at last learn to be thankful.

One day Elsie was preening her pretty feathers in the sunshine, and Mother brought her a big fat worm. Elsie took it, as usual, without saying "Thank you." And while she ate it she looked at Mother crossly.

"Mother, you look terrible," she said when she had swallowed the last bite. "I wish you'd fix yourself up and look a little neater. Your feathers are all rumpled and dull. Your toes are scaly and stained. I'm really ashamed of you. I would hate to have any of my friends meet you."

Mother Redbreast stared at her daughter in shocked surprise, and could not think what to say. She glanced down at her feathers and at her feet.

What Elsie said was true — she did look bedraggled and worn and shabby, and her feet were rough from much scratching for food. Busy as she was, feeding her family day after day, she hardly ever had time for washing in the pool, or preening her feathers in the sun.

Very sadly she said to Elsie, "Daughter, I've been busy caring for you and the other children. I'm sorry if I'm not good enough to be your mother."

Elsie should have hung her head in shame for herself, but instead she said, "Well, you could take care of yourself a little, so that I wouldn't have to be ashamed of you. Father, too, could dress up and take better care of himself. And besides that, your voice is harsh and rough; you do not talk sweetly, as you used to. And father doesn't sing any more."

Mrs. Redbreast turned away sadly, but Elsie had not finished. She called after her, "You see, mother, I'm meeting new friends every day, out here in Mrs. Duff's garden, and I want them to like me. But they won't want me as a friend if they see you looking so dowdy."

Mrs. Redbreast lifted her wings and flew away.

Just as her mother left, Elsie heard another flutter of wings in the bushes right above her head. She looked up in time to see a young robin flit to a higher branch. He was one of the very nicest of the young robins that came to the garden, and Elsie called to him.

"Its *you* they're ashamed of!" the beetle told
Elsie Redbreast.

Instead of coming to her, he flew to the nearest tree, and then away across the garden, as if he did not hear her.

All the rest of that day, and all the next day, Elsie did not meet any of her new friends. Or if she did meet them, they hardly spoke to her. They did not seem to want to be friends any more.

"It's because they saw my mother," Elsie told herself. "They are ashamed of me, because mother looks so worn and doesn't dress well."

She did not know she said that aloud, until a tiny sharp voice spoke right at her feet.

"You're all wrong, Miss Elsie," the voice said. "It's not your mother they are ashamed of. It's you!"

"Why, you horrid thing! Who are you? And what do you mean?" Elsie asked, looking all around.

"I'm right here," said the tiny sharp voice. "Right by your feet."

Then Elsie looked, and saw a big brown June beetle.

"What do you know about me?" she asked.

"Well," said the big June beetle, waving its feelers, "I happened to be up in yonder tree, resting, when you talked with your mother a few days ago, and a young robin was there too. Afterwards, I heard the young robin talk to the others. He said you weren't the sort of person to have for a friend. He said it was shameful, the way you talked to your mother. He said your manners were worse than her rumpled feathers. He said, 'Kindness and thoughtfulness are more important than fine feathers, and Elsie hasn't shown any kindness at all toward her mother.' He said, 'She thinks she's better than her mother, but she's not half as good!' That's why they don't want you for a friend, Miss Elsie!"

Elsie grew more and more angry as she listened to the June beetle. "Oh, you horrid thing!" she said at last. "I'll eat you for that!"

And she tried to pounce on the big brown beetle.

But the June beetle was too quick. It lifted its gauzy wings from under the brown covers and was gone.

"You'd better think it over!" it called over its shoulder.

Maybe Elsie will think it over, and mend her ways some day.

Bunny Rabbit peeked in.

8

Some Foolish Little Folk with Wings

THE midsummer sun shone day after day, so that even The Forest was very warm, and the pool almost dried up. But at night a little breeze came whispering through the treetops, and all the Forest Folk felt better.

Bunny Rabbit had rested at home much of the day, with his family. He always had a family. As soon as one set of children was grown up, another came along. When they were young, they needed only mother's milk, and then Bunny Rabbit could rest during the hot days. Besides, he would rather go out at night; it was not only cooler, but safer. And Farmer Duff's vegetables were more crisp after sundown.

One evening Bunny Rabbit went to Farmer Duff's garden, and nibbled lettuce until it was quite pitch dark. Then he started for home.

On the way, he had to pass Farmer Duff's house, and when he saw the lighted window of the living room, he stopped to look and listen. He could hear the voices of Farmer Duff and his children through the open window, but could not understand what they said.

Even when he went closer, he could not understand them. But he saw something on the window screen that made him look again and again. The screen was crowded with tiny little creatures of The Field and The Forest. They seemed to be having a picnic!

Dozens of moths were there, and lovely Lady Lacewing was there, and blundering Mrs. June Beetle, and sharp-tongued Mrs. Mosquito, and dandy Ben Firefly, besides a lot of folk Bunny Rabbit didn't know by name. They all seemed to be having fun.

But when Bunny looked closer, he noticed that every now and then one of the party would limp away with a broken wing or a broken leg. The rest kept right on dancing and playing; they didn't seem to notice that others were hurt.

Bunny Rabbit looked and looked. "A little fun and play is all right," he said to himself. "But these folk don't seem to do anything else but play. Even seeing others get hurt doesn't stop them."

After thinking a little, he decided that it was the light that kept them spellbound there. "They are creatures made for the light," he said, "and they don't know that the light of that window is artificial light. It does them no good at all. I shall go warn them that there is more to do in life than

play, and that there is a much better light to fly
to."

But when he came near the window, Bunny Rabbit saw something else that startled him still more.
In one corner of the window a spider had woven
a clever web. And he was hiding in the shadow,
waiting for a victim.

In his eagerness to warn them, Bunny Rabbit
called out, "Beware! Little foolish winged folk, beware! You are in danger!"

But no one listened. And at that very moment
a moth flew too close to the web; one wing caught
in the sticky threads. Quick as a wink, the spider
was upon the poor moth, and soon the poor thing
was tied tight with spider silk.

Bunny Rabbit wondered what the others would
do when they saw their friend captured by the spider, but not one took any notice of the poor moth.
They all went right on playing and dancing.

"Such foolish, foolish creatures," Bunny said
aloud, and once again he raised his voice to call a
warning to them.

Just then he saw someone move inside Farmer
Duff's house. He heard Farmer Duff say something,
very near the window. And he saw Farmer Duff's
arm move back and forth, as if he were pumping
something.

Immediately the little folk at the window began
tumbling down — dozens of them fell to the ground.
The moths, and Mrs. Mosquito, and lovely Lady

Lacewing, and Ben Firefly, and even Mr. Spider — they all fell down dead. Mrs. June Beetle and a few others dashed away madly, and escaped.

"They have poisoned us!" Mrs. June Beetle cried as she flew past Bunny.

And when Bunny sniffed the air, he smelled a strange odor — the odor of the poison Farmer Duff had sprayed against the screen. And Bunny Rabbit turned to run, too.

"Foolish little winged folk," he panted as he ran. "All they want to do is play and dance, by the lighted window, and this is what happens!"

They all sat in a row on the branch looking out
on the big wide world.

9

Little Fifth Chickadee

DEEP in the woods, in an old hollow tree, there lived the Chickadee Family — Mother Chickadee, Father Chickadee, and five little babies. Each one wore a grey coat, and a little black cap that came way down over his forehead, just letting the shiny black eyes peep out.

Mother and Father Chickadee were busy from morning till night, feeding the five little ones. But the little ones grew fast, and soon they were big enough to leave the nest.

"Come!" Mother Chickadee called from the doorway of the hollow tree. "Come out here, in the
sunshine, and learn to fly."

The baby chickadees had often wondered what
the outside world was like. All they could see of
it was a bit of sunshine peeking through the round
doorway.

So the first chickadee baby climbed up out of the
hollow log nest, and sat on the branch beside Mother
Chickadee. What a big, big world it was, all around
him! There were tall trees, with green leaves
swaying in the breeze; and high above, there was a
bright blue sky.

The second baby chickadee climbed out, too, and
sat beside his brother. Then the third one climbed
out, and the fourth, and at last the fifth. They all
sat in a row on the branch — five soft fluffy baby
chickadees, looking out on the big wide world.

For a time, Mother Chickadee let them sit there.
She and Father Chickadee brought them little bugs
and worms to eat.

But after a while Mother said, "Now you must
learn to fly. Come, follow me!" And she flew
to a branch just above their heads.

The first baby chickadee lifted his tiny wings
and fluttered up to the higher branch. The second one followed him. The third one flew up
there, too. And the fourth one. But the last one,
Little Fifth Chickadee, just sat very still on the
lower branch.

"Come!" said Mother Chickadee, and she held a little bug in her bill to tempt him.

But Little Fifth Chickadee would not even try to fly. "I can't!" he said. "I'm afraid. I'm afraid of the big wide world."

No matter how Mother coaxed, and Father commanded, Little Fifth Chickadee would not fly up to the higher branch.

"Well, we cannot wait for you," Mother Chickadee said. When she had fed them all once more she said, "Now come up higher yet, on the tiptop branch of the tree."

It was lovely up there, on the tiptop branch of the tree. The little birds could see the tops of other trees, and the far-away fields, and the white farmhouse up on the hill.

But Little Fifth Chickadee stayed alone, on the branch below. He huddled himself into a tiny ball of fuzz, and did not move.

Bit by bit Mother Chickadee coaxed her children on. She taught them how to catch bugs for themselves. She taught them how to hunt under every leaf and in all the little cracks of the tree bark, for that is where little bugs like to hide. Soon they were so far away that Little Fifth Chickadee could not hear their voices at all. But still he sat there, and would not move.

And then the sun went down, down, down in the west, and darkness began to creep over the woods.

Little Fifth Chickadee felt the darkness come, and he shivered. He lifted his head and looked around. Mother and Father were not in sight, nor were his brothers and sisters anywhere to be seen. He listened hard, but he could not even hear them.

The darkness came closer and closer. Little Fifth Chickadee huddled against the leaves. He was dreadfully lonely.

"Dee, dee, dee!" he called softly, hoping Mother would hear. He did not dare call louder, for fear some awful creature might be near by.

There was no answer.

Then it was very dark. Poor Little Fifth Chickadee tried to hide behind the leaves of the tree, so that they would be a curtain around him. But the leaves did not warm him, and he shivered again. He was used to sleeping under Mother's warm wings.

Little Fifth Chickadee shut his eyes and tucked his head under his little wing. He did not want to see the darkness. He wished he could go to sleep.

And then a terrible voice frightened him. It was a big voice near by, and it called out "Hoo-oo-oo-oo! Hoo-oo-oo-oo!"

"Oh, not me, not me!" Little Fifth Chickadee whispered, "Don't eat me!" And he tried to hide closer to the leaves. What if Mr. Owl should find him? Mr. Owl likes young chickadees for his midnight supper.

"Hoo-oo-oo-oo! Hoo-oo-oo-oo!" Mr. Owl called again. But the voice was farther away. And next time it was still farther away. After a while Little Fifth Chickadee did not hear it any more. Then he tucked his head under his wing again, and this time he fell asleep.

When Little Fifth Chickadee took his head from under his wing and opened his eyes, the sun was shining! The old owl was nowhere to be seen, and a robin was singing up in the top of the tree.

Little Fifth Chickadee stretched one little wing, and then the other little wing, till he was wide awake. He was glad the darkness was gone. But what must he do now?

"I'm hungry," he thought. "I must find something to eat."

But he had not watched mother teach the other baby chickadees. He did not know how to hunt under the leaves and in tiny cracks of bark. He could not find anything to eat at all.

Little Fifth Chickadee was feeling very hungry and very sorry when he heard a sound that made him lift his little head high, to listen. It seemed far away, but it came nearer, and it sounded very familiar. Was it Mother's voice? Could it be Mother's voice?

Yes, it was! Little Fifth Chickadee heard it clear as could be now, "Dee, dee, dee!"

With his own little voice, that shivered from cold and hunger, Little Fifth Chickadee answered her, "Dee, dee, dee! Here I am!"

And there she was, hopping and fluttering from branch to branch. The four other baby chickadees came fluttering along behind her, all chirping merrily.

"Oh, mother, mother!" Little Fifth Chickadee cried, "I'm sorry I was naughty! I'm sorry I didn't obey you! It was so awfully lonely and so awfully dark last night! And the big owl hooted very near me."

Mother Chickadee came and sat close beside her baby.

"You were afraid to come with me," she said. "You were afraid to do what was right. That is why I had to leave you alone through the dark night. You must never be afraid to do what you ought to do."

She stroked Little Fifth Chickadee's feathers with her bill, gently, and said, "Come now; fly with me, and I'll show you how to catch little bugs for your breakfast."

Then Little Fifth Chickadee followed her, along with his brothers and sisters, and he was happy.

"But I must remember," he said to himself, "never to be afraid to do what is right, never to be afraid to do what I ought to do, in the big wide world."

10

Reddy, The Squirrel

WARM autumn days are the loveliest days of all in The Forest. Then there is plenty of food for all the birds and animals. The air is fragrant with the perfume of ripe grapes, and the trees are laden with nuts.

All the Forest Folk were happy, but the happiest of all was Reddy, the Squirrel. He was very, very busy, too. Every day he hurried across the field to Farmer Duff's barn, and he hardly had time to chatter with the other Forest Folk.

One day Johnny Woodchuck called to him, as he leaped through the treetops along the edge of the creek.

"Hi there, Reddy! What are you so busy about?"

"Laying up my store of nuts for winter, of course," Reddy answered, without stopping.

"But why do you go to Farmer Duff's barn every day?" Johnny asked.

By this time Reddy was two trees away, and he only whisked his bushy tail and jumped to the next tree. He pretended not to hear.

"'Well, let him keep his secret," Johnny Woodchuck muttered to himself. And he went about the business of eating, to fatten himself for his long winter's sleep.

For all that, Johnny was curious to know what Reddy did at Farmer Duff's barn every day. And so were other Forest Folk. They watched him go and watched him come back, but they never saw him carry nuts. And he would not answer questions.

The beauty of Autumn lasted for many days. The Forest was gay with colored leaves — red and gold and yellow and brown. But one night old North Wind came riding swiftly from his summer home at the North Pole, and spoiled it all. He snatched the leaves off the trees and sent them flying left and right; he laughed and roared so loud and long that all the Forest Folk shivered in their beds.

After old North Wind, came Jack Frost; and after Jack Frost came the snow. One morning the Forest Folk wakened to find a white blanket covering the whole forest floor. A dainty pattern of snow was embroidered on every branch and twig of each tree.

Then Mr. and Mrs. Chipmunk crept into bed, to settle down for their winter's sleep. Mr. and Mrs. Woodchuck did the same. The Busy Bees huddled inside their hive, content to stay in a warm place with plenty of honey to eat. Polly dug deep into the mud at the edge of the pond, and curled

"I'm so angry I could bite my tail off," wailed Reddy.

up to sleep there. Mr. and Mrs. Redbreast, and all the other robins, had already flown to the Southland.

But Bunny Rabbit did not mind the snow at all. He hopped around in it, warm and comfortable in his good fur coat, and nosed around for a bit of green to nibble on. And then it was that he found out about Reddy's secret.

Reddy was in the top of the elm tree, jerking his tail, jumping from one branch to another without going anywhere, and scolding in a very sharp, angry voice.

Bunny Rabbit looked up at him, and then glanced around to see who was getting the scolding. But there was no one else in sight.

"What's the matter?" he called at last.

Reddy's tail began jerking even more furiously and he came down the tree at top speed. Bunny was almost afraid. But Reddy stopped on the branch just above Bunny's head.

"What's the matter?" he repeated. "Everything is! I am so angry that I could bite my own tail off. How could I be so foolish! So terribly foolish! If I had only looked into the matter more carefully! Oh dear, oh dear!"

He looked so terribly upset that Bunny Rabbit felt sorry for him.

"Do tell me about it," he said. "Maybe I can help you."

"I'm sure you can't help," said Reddy. "But I'll tell you. If I don't tell somebody, I'm afraid I'll burst. It was a secret — a beautiful secret. But it turned out all wrong!"

Bunny sat still, waiting for Reddy to go on, and Reddy calmed himself as best he could to tell the story.

It was during those beautiful autumn days, he told Bunny, that he happened to find a black walnut tree on Farmer Duff's land, and the tree was loaded with nuts. Besides that, he found a big box in the shed behind Farmer Duff's barn — a box with a hole in the top, a hole just big enough to drop the nuts in. It was a perfect storage place for his treasure of nuts.

"I spent days and days filling that box with nuts," said Reddy. "I was so proud and so happy. And now . . ."

At the very thought, Reddy shivered from head to foot, and jerked his tail till he almost fell off the branch.

"Did Farmer Duff take the box away, perhaps?" Bunny asked.

"No, no!" said Reddy. "If it were that, I could blame Farmer Duff. But I have only myself to blame. I was so very, very foolish. I discovered it just this morning. Because the ground is all covered with snow, I thought I would go over to my treasure and enjoy a few nuts. There's enough to last me all winter. But when I got there . . ."

Reddy stopped again, as if he just could not bear to tell the rest.

"Did someone discover your secret, and steal them?" Bunny asked.

"No, no!" said Reddy. "They are all there. All the nuts I gathered are in the treasure box. But I can't get one of them out! Not one! The hole is too small for me to get through, and I can't even reach one of them! And the wood is thick and hard — much too hard to nibble through. And the box is too heavy to tip over!"

Bunny stared at poor Reddy with great sympathy. What a pity!

"Can't you think of some way to get the box open?" he asked at last. "Maybe there's another hole."

Reddy sighed. "I've tried everything," he said. "And I'm sure there isn't anything you can do to help, Bunny Rabbit. Farmer Duff could open it, but I can't ask him to. I've been very foolish, and I'll have to suffer for my own foolishness."

Very slowly and sadly Reddy turned to climb back up the tree.

Bunny Rabbit watched him. "What a pity," he said. "All that time spent in storing up treasures, and then losing all. We certainly ought to be careful where we lay up our treasures! Poor Reddy has only himself to blame, as he says."

11

Crickie, The Violinist

ALL through the warm summer days, Crickie the Cricket had been one of the cheeriest of all the Forest Folk. From morning till night, and often through the night, he played his violin. Sometimes he played for hours and hours, without stopping except for a bite to eat.

Folks said that Crickie did not amount to much. He never did any great deeds; he was shy, and hid under leaves and grass most of the time. But he and his relatives add great cheer to The Forest every summer. What a quiet place The Forest would be if there were no crickets to strum their violins!

Nosing around in the early snow for his lunch on a cold day, Bunny Rabbit noticed that The Forest was very quiet, and suddenly he realized that the crickets were all gone. Jack Frost had killed them, and silenced their music.

"That's a pity," he said to himself. "They were such cheery fellows. But good cheer and happiness last only a short time. There is so much trouble in life, it is a wonder we can be happy at all."

He hopped along toward Sunny Bank, and there he found the snow nearly gone. The sun had melted it, and had warmed up the forest floor a bit. And there, to his surprise, he heard the sound of a cricket's violin.

Bunny Rabbit had to listen carefully, for the sound of the violin was quite feeble and faint. But it surely was there.

"Crickie!" Bunny Rabbit called. "Crickie! Are you still alive? Where are you hiding?"

"I'm right here, against this brown log," Crickie's weak voice answered. "The sun shone on the log, and has warmed me up a bit."

Bunny Rabbit hopped closer, and there he found Crickie, huddled against the brown log, softly strumming his violin. The shiny wing covers moved slowly, shivering a little as they scraped out the music.

"It's good to hear you," said Bunny Rabbit. "But Crickie, you must have been nearly frozen to death. How can you keep on playing?"

Crickie shifted his shiny black body so that the sun would warm him better, and answered, "It's true, these cold nights make me stiffer and stiffer, so that my strumming is slower and slower; and soon I shall have to stop altogether. But I won't stop before I have to. Why should I? My Maker gave me a violin, and a cheery song of praise to strum on it, and I shall keep at my task till I die. That's what I am here for!"

"But your life is so short. And it must be horrid to freeze to death," said Bunny Rabbit.

"What does it matter if my life is short?" Crickie asked. "I shall make my music until my wing covers are too stiff to move."

Crickie was huddled against the brown log,
softly strumming his violin.

Lifting one wing cover and then the other, he rubbed them together, "Creek, crick; creek, crick."

Bunny Rabbit watched him with great admiration.

"You are right," he said. "I wish I could live so bravely and cheerfully, and so unafraid."

"You can," said Crickie.

"Maybe I can," Bunny Rabbit said to himself as he hopped away. "I'm sure we all ought to. Life is short, and full of troubles. But that doesn't matter. It's how we live it — it's our courage and faith and cheer that matter."

12

Who's Afraid?

JACK FROST came night after night, and he took hold of everything in The Forest. He stripped the leaves off every tree except the oak, and left the trees standing bare and stiff. He silenced the babbling creek by covering it with a coat of ice; and he froze the pond, too.

Most of the furry folk of The Forest were asleep in their nests by that time, and were glad when the clouds brought a blanket of snow and laid it over them gently. Most all the birds had now flown south. Jack Frost had killed the crickets and the katydids and the grasshoppers; the bees were in their hives. So The Forest was a very quiet place.

But a few of the Forest Folk were still awake. There was Reddy, the Squirrel; he slept part of the time, but when the weather was good he was out hunting nuts, and he liked to climb the trees and shake the snow down. And there were a few birds that dared to stay through the cold winter. Downy Woodpecker stayed, and Nutty the Nuthatch, and Tufty the Titmouse, and all the Chickadees. They were very busy every day, hunting for little bits of food tucked in the bark of the trees.

As they hunted, they always called to each other in cheery voices. The chickadees were especially merry, and without them The Forest would have been very, very quiet indeed.

One day the chickadees wandered near to Farmer Duff's house, to hunt little insect eggs in Farmer Duff's orchard. And there they saw The Boy and The Girl out in the snow. The Boy carried a hammer, and The Girl carried a strange wooden thing that looked like a box open on one side.

Now Little Fifth Chickadee had grown up, and was not afraid any more. So he flew to the tree nearest to The Boy and The Girl, to watch them. He saw them put the strange box-shelf on a post and nail it down tight. And he saw them put something on it.

As soon as The Boy and The Girl were gone, Little Fifth Chickadee flew over to investigate. He was curious, and wanted to know what this thing might be. First he landed on top of the box, and then he peeked into it, and to his surprise he saw a wonderful heap of sunflower seeds lying there! There was a chunk of suet, too, fastened to one side of the box-shelf.

Now chickadees are very fond of sunflower seeds, so Little Fifth Chickadee quickly took one and flew away with it. Perched in a nearby tree, he tucked the seed under his little toes, and began to peck at

Every morning they found a fresh supply
of their daily bread.

it with his sharp little bill. Bits of the shell flew to right and left, till the kernel was uncovered. Little Fifth Chickadee ate the sweet kernel, and it tasted so good that he wanted more!

Back and forth Little Fifth Chickadee went, eating one sunflower seed after the other.

When the other chickadees saw their brother feasting on sunflower seeds, they came to get their share. Tufty came, too. And Nutty came. And Downy came to peck at the suet.

By the time the winter sun was ready for bed, the sunflower seeds were gone!

The very next morning, Little Fifth Chickadee crept out of his bed in the evergreen tree and hurried right over to see if there were more seeds on the shelf-box. There were! Little Fifth Chickadee was just in time to see The Girl put them there.

That day he feasted again, and so did all the other winter birds. From then on, the shelf-box became their winter dining table. Every evening it was empty. But every morning they found a fresh supply of their daily bread. No wonder the winter birds of The Forest were happy!

But one morning when Little Fifth Chickadee came to the shelf, there were no seeds there — not even one. Little Fifth Chickadee was quite disappointed, and was just opening his mouth to scold, when the door of Farmer Duff's house opened, and out came The Girl.

But The Girl did not put seeds on the shelf. Instead, she stood near the shelf and held out her hand, and her hand was full of seeds. Meanwhile she looked right at Little Fifth Chickadee, and made a little noise with her lips — a noise that sounded like an invitation.

Now Little Fifth Chickadee was hungry. And he had learned that The Girl did not mean to hurt him. So he wanted to go and take a seed right out of her hand. But he did not quite dare.

Little Fifth Chickadee sat very still up in the tree, looking at the handful of seeds. The Girl stood very still, waiting.

At last Little Fifth Chickadee flew down toward her. But when he came near her, he lost his courage; he flew past. Again and again he flew past her, very close. She did not move at all. And then at last he did it — he flew to her hand, he grabbed a seed, and he flew away as fast as he could!

After that, Little Fifth Chickadee was not afraid of The Girl any more. Whenever he saw her, he flew to her, and she gave him sunflower seeds.

But one day Reddy happened to be in a nearby tree, and Reddy saw Little Fifth Chickadee take a seed from The Girl's hand.

Reddy stared in amazement, and then called out, "No, no! You foolish chickadee! Don't do that! You'll get hurt!"

"I'm not afraid," Little Fifth Chickadee answered, as he flew to the tree with the seed.

"But you should be afraid," said Reddy. "All the animals of The Forest are afraid of People."

"The Girl and The Boy do not hurt us," said Little Fifth Chickadee. "Watch me when I go for another seed. I will sit right on her hand and talk to her."

Reddy watched with wonder, as Little Fifth Chickadee flew to The Girl and perched on her hand. The tiny bird looked right up into The Girl's face and said, "Dee, dee, dee!"

When he came back with a seed, Reddy jerked his tail and scolded. "You are taking a terrible risk," he said.

But Little Fifth Chickadee answered, "The Boy and The Girl are not like many other people. They are kind to us."

Reddy flicked his tail thoughtfully. He could not understand. He was sure all the Forest Folk should be afraid of People. Nobody had ever told him that it was not so in the beginning, or that there was once a time when none of the animals were afraid of man.

He wished he could have some of those sunflower seeds. But he didn't dare take one from The Girl's hand. He flicked his tail again, and then scampered away through the treetops.

Meanwhile Little Fifth Chickadee flew back to get another seed from The Girl. He wasn't afraid. He was happy.

But there was something, too, that Chickadee didn't know. He didn't know that some day there will be a new heaven and a new earth, more beautiful than this one, with no fear, no danger, and no sorrow at all!

There is so much that the Forest Folk do not know. They do not know that all the troubles of this earth have come because of sin. They do not know that God sent Jesus, His Son, to bear the punishment of sin, and to redeem God's wonderful creation. They do not even know that God made them, to live in The Forest and glorify Him.

But we know, because we can read God's Book. And when we watch the little Forest Folk that God made, we learn many lessons from them. We'll be glad when spring comes to wake them up, to make The Forest a busy place again.